Please return on or before the latest date above.
You can renew online at www.kent.gov.uk/libs
or by phone 08458 247 200

CUSTOMER SERVICE EXCELLENCE

Libraries & Archives

D1439522

C555095319

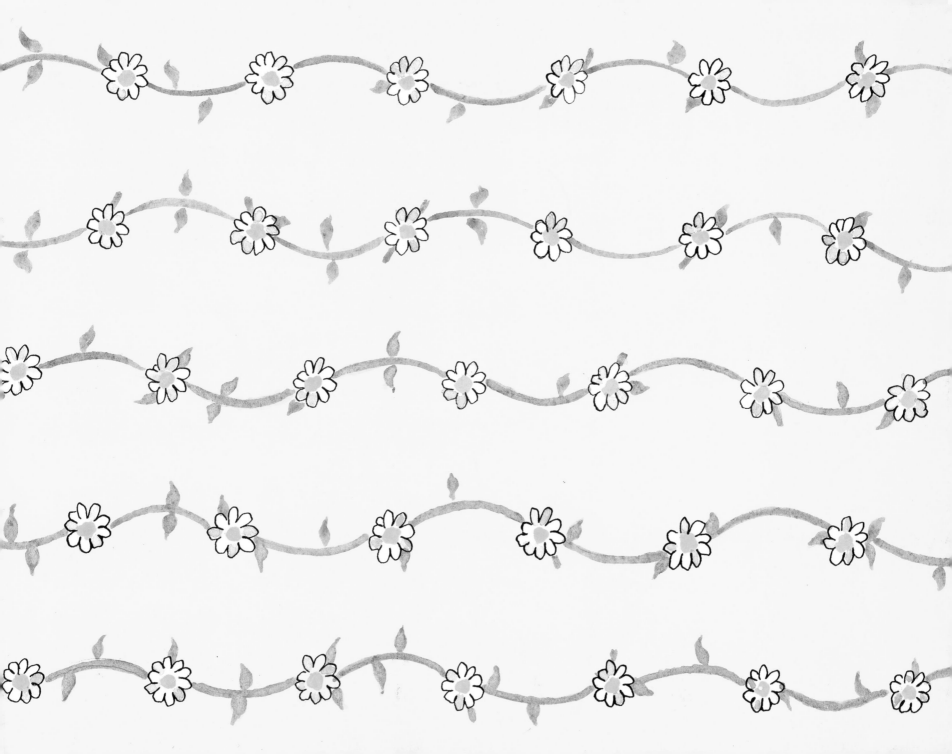

To Daisy and Rosie
love Mij

For Alison – Nicholas

First published in 2011
by Hodder Children's Books
This paperback edition
first published in 2012

Text copyright © Mij Kelly 2011
Illustrations copyright © Nicholas Allan 2011

Hodder Children's Books
338 Euston Road
London NW1 3BH

Hodder Children's Books Australia
Level 17/207 Kent Street
Sydney NSW 2000

A catalogue record of this book is available from the British Library.

ISBN: 978 0 340 98950 0
10 9 8 7 6 5 4 3 2 1

Printed in China

Hodder Children's Books is a division
of Hachette Children's Books.
An Hachette UK Company
www.hachette.co.uk

The
Bump

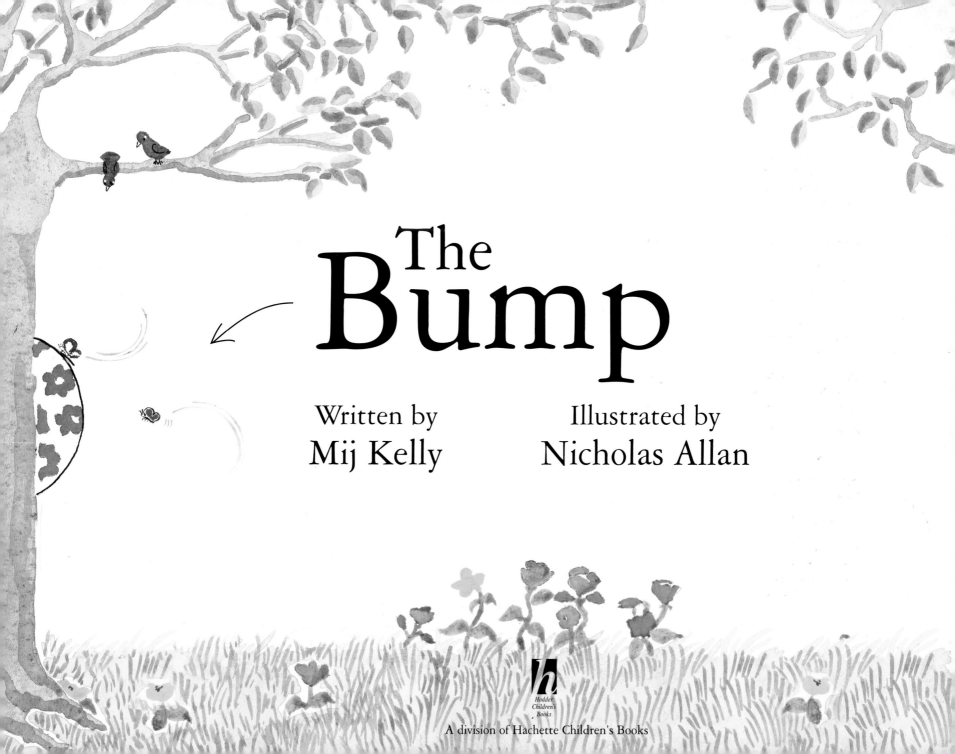

Written by
Mij Kelly

Illustrated by
Nicholas Allan

Hodder Children's Books

A division of Hachette Children's Books

This is a story about someone you know
and something that happened a few years ago,
before she was famous for loving you
and for hip-hip-hooraying the things that you do
and mopping your spills and kissing you better…

… it's about your mummy before you met her.

The story begins on the day her world changed.
She felt a bit sick and a little bit strange.

Then, all of a sudden, her heart gave a thump,
when she looked in the mirror and noticed a bump.

Well maybe she felt a little bit scared,
very excited and not quite prepared,

but right then and there she whispered, "Hello",
and felt her love begin to grow.

Then out she went into the sun
to show the bump to everyone,

and dress it up in daisy chains
and think of extra-special names
for the bump.

She treasured the bump like she treasures you,
and the bump – like her love – grew and grew.

It grew and grew like anything
until her buttons all went… PING!

So she bought a humungous tent to wear,
a flowery tent for the bump to share,

NEW!

Peppermint
&
Onion

Ice cream!

and ate apples and peaches and other good things
(plus green ice cream and onion rings) for the bump.

She looked after the bump
like she looks after you,
and the bump – like her love
– grew and grew.

It grew so very big and stout
that games of hide-and-seek
were out!

She showed the doctor her marvellous bump
and heard its heart going **thumpitty-thump**...

… and saw the baby hiding inside
and laughed out loud and almost cried.

The picture they gave her exists today –
she kept it safely tucked away.

THE GREAT SANDCASTL

She cherished that bump like she cherishes you,
and the bump – like her love – grew and grew.

It grew to such a stupendous size
that she accidentally won a prize!

BiG BiB

She hugged it and lugged it all across town.
She never once stopped and put that bump down,
but rushed about in search of things
like stripy socks and teething rings
and vests and hats and itsy mits…

Bigger Bib

The Bump

… she even tried to learn to knit.

She cared for the bump like she cares for you,
and the bump – like her love – grew and grew.

It grew till the baby curled up inside
was suddenly far too big to hide.

This is a story about someone you know
and something that happened a few years ago.

It happened the day the baby unfurled
and came out of the bump and into the world.

And maybe you felt a little bit scared,
very excited and not quite prepared...

... but there was your mummy saying, "Hello!"
with a love for you that grows and grows.

And now you're walking on your own,
just look how **big** her love has **grown!**

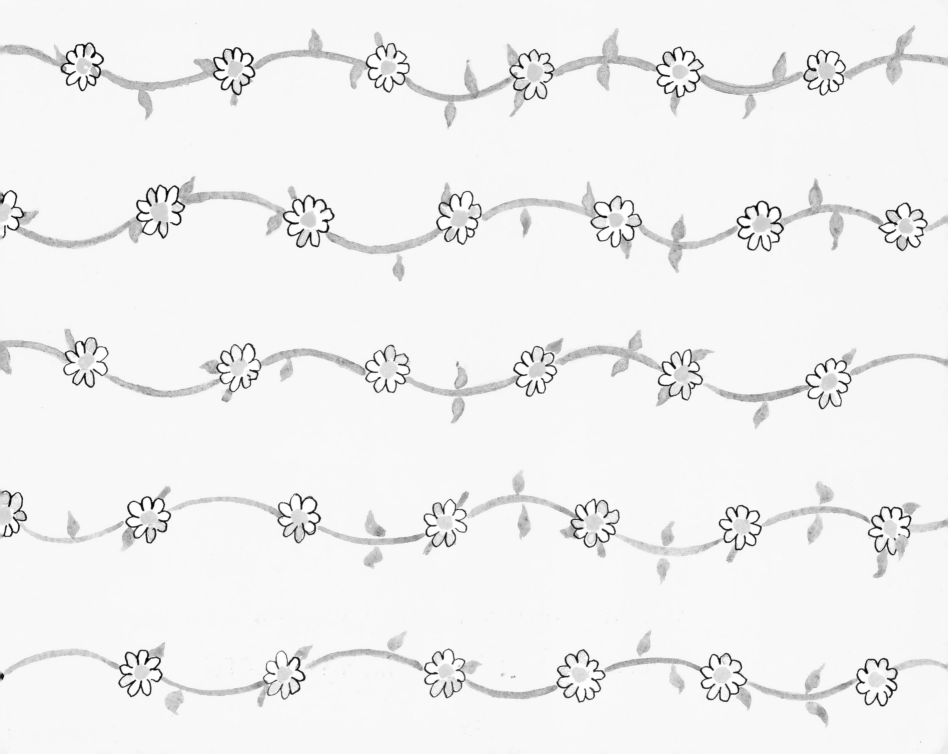

If you enjoyed this book, you'll love:

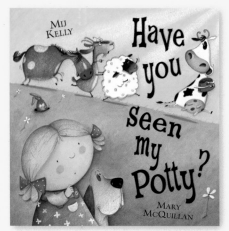

978 0 340 91153 2

978 0 340 94526 1

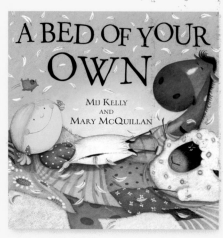

978 0 340 99928 8

978 0 340 95691 5

978 0 340 96000 4

978 0 340 89331 9